Hansel
and Gretel

First published in 2008 by
Franklin Watts
338 Euston Road
London
NW1 3BH

Franklin Watts Australia
Level 17/207 Kent Street
Sydney
NSW 2000

A CIP catalogue record for this book is available
from the British Library.

ISBN 978 0 7496 7898 2 (hbk)
ISBN 978 0 7496 7904 0 (pbk)

Series Editor: Melanie Palmer
Series Advisor: Dr Barrie Wade
Series Designer: Peter Scoulding

Printed in China

Franklin Watts is a division of
Hachette Children's Books,
an Hachette Livre UK company.

HOPSCOTCH
FAIRY TALES

Hansel
and Gretel

by Anne Walter and David Lopez

W
FRANKLIN WATTS
LONDON•SYDNEY

Once, two children called Hansel
and Gretel lived with their father
and stepmother near the woods.

The family was very poor.

"Take the children to the woods,
there is no food left for them here,"
said the stepmother.

Sadly, the father led his children into the woods. "Try to find some food here," he said. Then he crept away.

"How will we find our way home?"
Gretel asked. Hansel took out his
last crust of bread.

"I will drop these breadcrumbs as we walk," Hansel said. "We can follow them back home later."

They walked deep into the woods.

Soon they were tired and hungry.

"Let's go home," said Gretel.

But when Hansel looked behind him, the breadcrumbs had gone! "Oh no!" he cried, "We're lost!"

So Hansel and Gretel kept walking.
They walked until they could walk
no more.

Suddenly they saw a house and
ran towards it.

"Look!" cried Hansel, "the roof is made of gingerbread!"

14

"And the door is *ALL* chocolate!"
said Gretel, munching greedily.
They ate and ate until ...

CREAK! The cottage door opened.
"You poor children," said a little old
lady, smiling. "How hungry you are!
There's plenty more food inside."

So Hansel raced into the cottage
and Gretel followed.

Then, SLAM! The little old lady shut the door and laughed a wicked laugh. She was really a witch!

"Now you have eaten my house,
I am going to eat you!" she cried.
Hansel and Gretel were scared.

"But you're both too thin to eat,"
the witch growled, pinching them.
"I'll have to fatten you up first."

The witch fed them every day.
She made Gretel work hard and
locked Hansel in a cage so they
could not escape.

The witch could not see very well.
She felt Hansel's finger to check
how fat he was. When Gretel saw
this, she made a plan.

"Hansel, hold out this chicken bone instead of your finger. It is much thinner," whispered Gretel.

"Still too thin!" shouted the witch
as she grabbed the chicken bone.

The witch grew tired of waiting.

"I will eat you now!" she cried.

"Get in that oven, girl!"

"But I'm too big" said Gretel.

"Nonsense," said the witch.

"Even *I* can fit inside there!"

"How?" asked Gretel, cleverly.

"Silly girl, like this," the witch said.

Gretel rushed to the oven door
and slammed it shut. The witch
was trapped inside.

Then Gretel unlocked the cage and
let Hansel out. They were free!

The witch's house was full of treasure! Hansel and Gretel filled their pockets with jewels and went to find their father.

When they got home, Father was delighted. Their stepmother had left and he had been looking for them. They all lived happily ever after.

Hopscotch has been specially designed to fit the requirements of the Literacy Framework. It offers real books by top authors and illustrators for children developing their reading skills. There are 55 Hopscotch stories to choose from:

Marvin, the Blue Pig
ISBN 978 0 7496 4619 6

Plip and Plop
ISBN 978 0 7496 4620 2

The Queen's Dragon
ISBN 978 0 7496 4618 9

Flora McQuack
ISBN 978 0 7496 4621 9

Willie the Whale
ISBN 978 0 7496 4623 3

Naughty Nancy
ISBN 978 0 7496 4622 6

Run!
ISBN 978 0 7496 4705 6

The Playground Snake
ISBN 978 0 7496 4706 3

"Sausages!"
ISBN 978 0 7496 4707 0

Bear in Town
ISBN 978 0 7496 5875 5

Pippin's Big Jump
ISBN 978 0 7496 4710 0

Whose Birthday Is It?
ISBN 978 0 7496 4709 4

The Princess and the Frog
ISBN 978 0 7496 5129 9

Flynn Flies High
ISBN 978 0 7496 5130 5

Clever Cat
ISBN 978 0 7496 5131 2

Moo!
ISBN 978 0 7496 5332 3

Izzie's Idea
ISBN 978 0 7496 5334 7

Roly-poly Rice Ball
ISBN 978 0 7496 5333 0

I Can't Stand It!
ISBN 978 0 7496 5765 9

Cockerel's Big Egg
ISBN 978 0 7496 5767 3

How to Teach a Dragon Manners
ISBN 978 0 7496 5873 1

The Truth about those Billy Goats
ISBN 978 0 7496 5766 6

Marlowe's Mum and the Tree House
ISBN 978 0 7496 5874 8

The Truth about Hansel and Gretel
ISBN 978 0 7496 4708 7

The Best Den Ever
ISBN 978 0 7496 5876 2

ADVENTURE STORIES

Aladdin and the Lamp
ISBN 978 0 7496 6692 7

Blackbeard the Pirate
ISBN 978 0 7496 6690 3

George and the Dragon
ISBN 978 0 7496 6691 0

Jack the Giant-Killer
ISBN 978 0 7496 6693 4

TALES OF KING ARTHUR

1. The Sword in the Stone
ISBN 978 0 7496 6694 1

2. Arthur the King
ISBN 978 0 7496 6695 8

3. The Round Table
ISBN 978 0 7496 6697 2

4. Sir Lancelot and the Ice Castle
ISBN 978 0 7496 6698 9

TALES OF ROBIN HOOD

Robin and the Knight
ISBN 978 0 7496 6699 6

Robin and the Monk
ISBN 978 0 7496 6700 9

Robin and the Silver Arrow
ISBN 978 0 7496 6703 0

Robin and the Friar
ISBN 978 0 7496 6702 3

FAIRY TALES

The Emperor's New Clothes
ISBN 978 0 7496 7421 2

Cinderella
ISBN 978 0 7496 7417 5

Snow White
ISBN 978 0 7496 7418 2

Jack and the Beanstalk
ISBN 978 0 7496 7422 9

The Three Billy Goats Gruff
ISBN 978 0 7496 7420 5

The Pied Piper of Hamelin
ISBN 978 0 7496 7419 9

Goldilocks and the Three Bears
ISBN 978 0 7496 7897 5 *
ISBN 978 0 7496 7903 3

Hansel and Gretel
ISBN 978 0 7496 7898 2 *
ISBN 978 0 7496 7904 0

The Three Little Pigs
ISBN 978 0 7496 7899 9 *
ISBN 978 0 7496 7905 7

Rapunzel
ISBN 978 0 7496 7900 2 *
ISBN 978 0 7496 7906 4

Little Red Riding Hood
ISBN 978 0 7496 7901 9 *
ISBN 978 0 7496 7907 1

Rumpelstiltskin
ISBN 978 0 7496 7902 6*
ISBN 978 0 7496 7908 8

HISTORIES

Toby and the Great Fire of London
ISBN 978 0 7496 7410 6

Pocahontas the Peacemaker
ISBN 978 0 7496 7411 3

Grandma's Seaside Bloomers
ISBN 978 0 7496 7412 0

Hoorah for Mary Seacole
ISBN 978 0 7496 7413 7

Remember the 5th of November
ISBN 978 0 7496 7414 4

Tutankhamun and the Golden Chariot
ISBN 978 0 7496 7415 1

* hardback